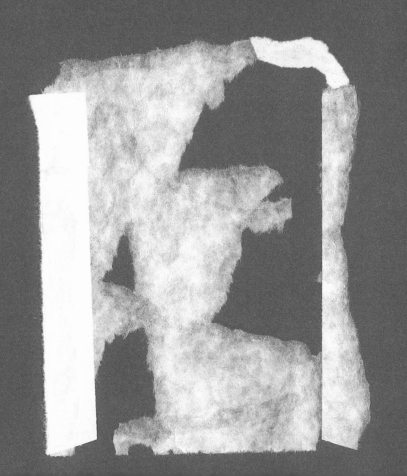

EVE MERRIAM

THE CHRISTMAS BOX

ILLUSTRATED BY DAVID SMALL

WILLIAM MORROW AND COMPANY, INC.
NEW YORK

3   4   5   6   7   8   9   10

Library of Congress Cataloging in Publication Data: Merriam, Eve, 1916–   The Christmas box.
Summary: Eager to see all the presents, the family comes downstairs on Christmas morning to find just
one long thin box under the tree. 1. Children's stories, American. [1. Christmas—Fiction]
I. Small, David, 1945–   ill. II. Title.   PZ7.M543Ch   1985   [E]   85-5666
ISBN 0-688-05255-X
ISBN 0-688-05256-8 (lib. bdg.)

For Colette and Danny
—E.M.

To Sherry
—D.S.

It was early, very early on Christmas morning, and the whole family was awake and eager to see all the presents that Santa had left under the tree.

Grandmother handed Grandfather his glasses.
Then Grandfather handed Grandmother hers.

Mother left the bed unmade
and didn't even brush her hair.

Father left the top
off the toothpaste tube.

Jasper tied a broken fishing line
around his bathrobe. Whiskers had
scampered off with the belt.

Belinda slid down the banister.
Louis jumped down the stairs two at a time.
The twins, Wilma and Waldo,
bumped their way down backward.

Aunt Elma held the baby high over her head to gurgle at the shiny star on top of the tree. It was a dark green fir that still smelled of the forest, of spicy ferns and clear spring water and birds darting through the branches. A perfect nesting place for all the presents.

Whose package would be opened first?

Under the tree there was a long, thin box.

And that was all.

Everyone looked
around the tree,
around the room,
in the hall,
up the chimney,

out on the porch,
even in the garage
and the mailbox.

There was nothing more.
Just one long, thin box.

Nobody wanted to open it.

Then Whiskers climbed up onto the box and clawed at the wrapping. The baby crawled over and began pulling at the ribbon.

So it had to be opened.

And inside there was...

a fishing rod and line for Jasper,

and attached to the end of the fishing line there was . . .

a telescope for Mother,
and attached to one end of the telescope there was . . .

a concertina for Father to play,
and attached to the far end of the concertina there was. . .

a striped umbrella for Grandfather,
and attached to the handle of the umbrella there was . . .

a flute for Grandmother,
and threaded through the top hole on the flute there was. . .

a kite string for a rainbow kite for Belinda,
and attached to the tail of the rainbow kite there was . . .

a hammock for Aunt Elma,
and attached to the end of the hammock there was. . .

a bow and arrow for Louis,
and attached to the tip
of the arrow there was. . .

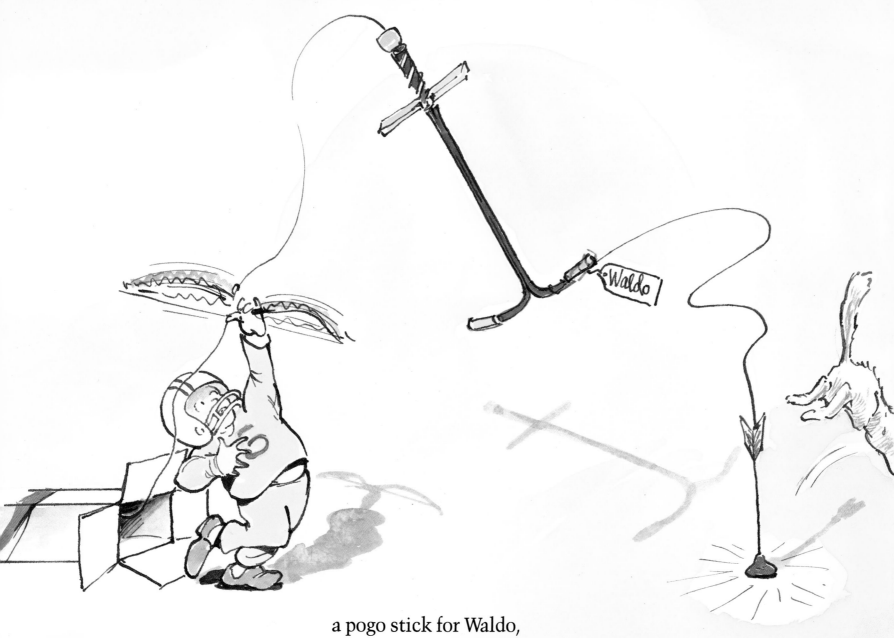

a pogo stick for Waldo,
and attached to the pogo stick there was. . .

a set of toy trains for Wilma,
and attached to the caboose there was. . .

a mother duck with her ducklings for Baby,
and attached to the last of the ducklings there was. . .

a ball of yarn
with a tiny
catnip mouse
for Whiskers.

And everyone had a merry merry,

jolly jolly, happy happy holiday.